Isabella Abnormella

and the Very, Very Finicky Queen of Trouble

J. PATRICK LEWIS

ILLUSTRATIONS BY

KYRSTEN BROOKER

DORLING KINDERSLEY PUBLISHING, INC.

*For Donna Marple
and Patti Welch,
the Princess and
the Queen
Ain't No Mountain High
Enough* —J.P.L.

*For Alex and Marcus,
with love* —K.B.

A Melanie Kroupa Book

DK
Ink

Dorling Kindersley Publishing, Inc.
95 Madison Avenue, New York, New York 10016
Visit us on the World Wide Web at http://www.dk.com

Dorling Kindersley books are available at special
discounts for bulk purchases for sales promotions or
premiums. Special editions, including personalized covers,
excerpts of existing guides, and corporate imprints can
be created in large quantities for specific needs. For
more information, contact Special Markets Dept.,
Dorling Kindersley Publishing, Inc., 95 Madison
Avenue, New York, New York 10016;
fax: (800) 600-9098.

Library of Congress Cataloging-in-Publication Data
Lewis, J. Patrick.
Isabella Abnormella and the very, very finicky Queen
of Trouble/by J. Patrick Lewis;
illustrated by Kyrsten Brooker. — 1st ed.   p.   cm.
"A Melanie Kroupa book."
  Summary: When the Queen of Trouble cannot sleep
  because all the beds she tries are uncomfortable,
  Isabella Abnormella saves the day by inventing the
  water bed.   ISBN 0-7894-2605-6
  [1. Water beds (Furniture)—Fiction. 2. Beds—Fiction.
  3. Sleep—Fiction. 4. Kings, queens, rulers, etc.—Fiction.
  5. Stories in rhyme.]   I. Brooker, Kyrsten, ill.
  II. Title.   PZ8.3.L5855Is   2000   [E]—dc21
  99-14755   CIP

Book design by Chris Hammill Paul
The illustrations for this book were created using
collage and oil paint.
The text of this book is set in 14 point Caxton Book.
Printed and bound in U.S.A.

First edition, 2000
10 9 8 7 6 5 4 3 2 1

The town of Trouble lay between
Good-Grief! and Who's-to-Blame?—
Three villages exactly almost
Opposite the same.

The folks of Trouble couldn't count
The troubles they had seen
Because of all the pouting by
Her Majesty, the Queen.

In her knickerbocker nightgown
And her periwinkle cap,
She'd tiptoe to the Twinkle Room—
Her chambers—for a nap.

No comforters, plush pillows,
Sheets of silk or velveteen
Could bring a golden slumber
To Her Majesty, the Queen.

Not a moment's fitful dozing,
Not a wink from counting sheep,
Night and day she'd toss and turn
Without one dreamy dream of sleep.

So she pouted at the poodles
And she pouted at the Prince.
And she pouted when the servants set out
Heart-shaped pillow mints.

She pouted from the parlor,
Kitchen, garden, balconies,
At weddings and at funerals
And on anniversaries.

One evening as she pitter-
Pattered round the Royal Loft,
She cried, "My Royal Mattress
is too hard, or else . . .

too soft!

Is it too much to request—
After all, I am the Queen—
That I'd like a little rest
On a bed that's . . . *in between*?"

So the maid informed the butler,
Who ran to tell the King
Of the Queen of Trouble's troubles
With the mattress and the spring.

"Soft or hard?" announced the butler,
"It's impossible to find
A mattress to impress Her Lady's
Delicate behind!"

The King he listened carefully
(The King's a careful man),
Then sliding down the banister,
He hatched a brilliant plan.

"Good citizens of Trouble,
Will you gather round the moat?
Your Queen's extremely restless—
I suggest we take a vote!

Shall I sleep her in a casket?
Or the gardener's wheelbarrow?

An enormous wicker basket,
Not too wide, but not too narrow?

Shall I swing her from a hammock?
Bounce her on a trampoline?

Shall I drop a quarter in
My Mister Tickle Dream Machine?

Shall I roll her on a gurney?

Shall I pitch the palace tent?

Do your duty, troubled voters,
FOR THE SAKE OF GOV-ERN-MENT!"

And then it was that I stepped forth
To say what *I* would do.
"I'm Isabella Abnormella
Pinkerton McPugh."

"Excuse me, Isabella Abnormella . . .
Uhh . . . Mc*Who*?"
The King could not believe his ears,
"Now who, pray tell, are *you*?"

"I'm Keeper of the Royal Cat,
Your Royal Highness, sir,
And I'll invent a Royal Cot
That makes Her Highness purr.

Queen Angeline might well prefer
A bed that's cool and wavy,
Like bubble baths or like the seas
That float the Royal Navy.
Something soothing, soft and deep . . .
Why, she'd slumber like a baby."

And so I had a gunnysack
Sewn twenty times as large

And filled with water from the moat.
(I put the King in charge!)

And the ending to this story,
As the history books have said,
Was the wonderful invention of . . .

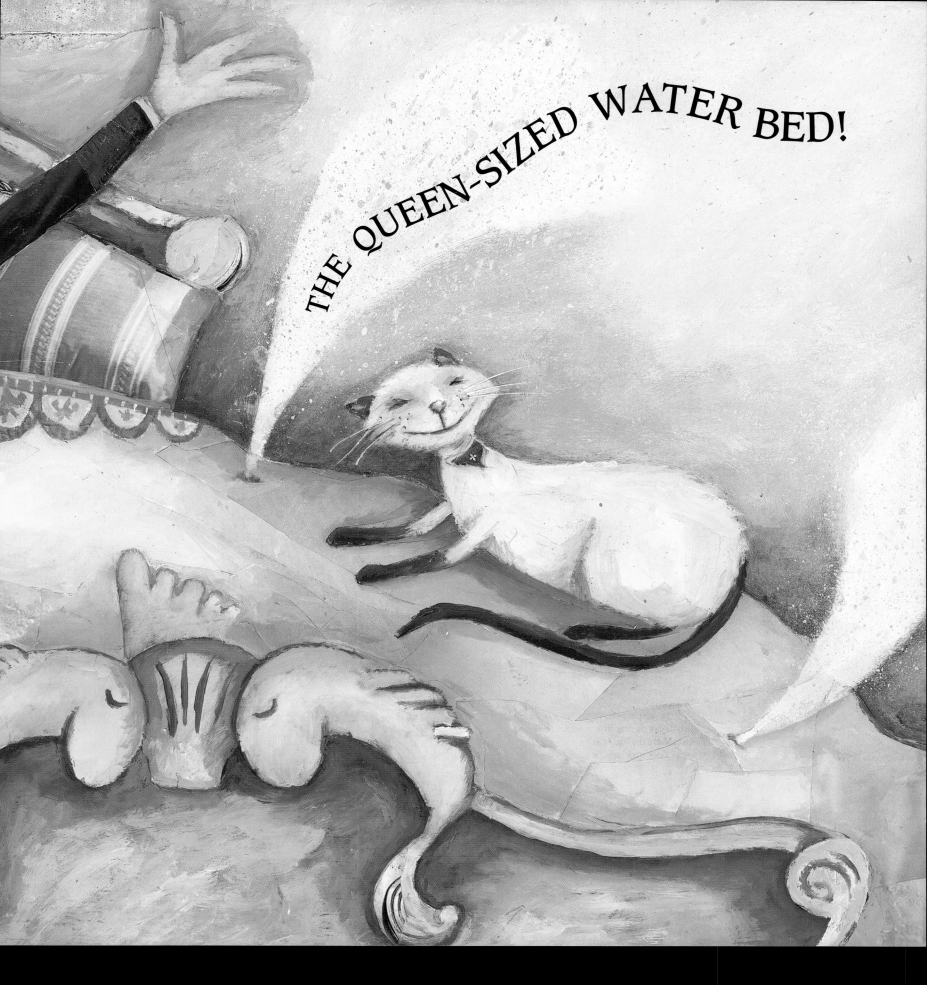

Good-Grief! and Who's-to-Blame? still meet
With trouble now and then,
But in the town of Trouble trouble
Never rose again.

And I have since become the King
And Queen's adopted daughter,
Who helped to save the kingdom
Just because I mentioned . . .

WATER!